Ready for

by Carol Pugliano-Martin

illustrated by Lynn Avril-Cravath

Meet the Characters

Elmwood Tree

the children

Flapper Bird

The air was warm. Elmwood Tree's branches were full of leaves. Summer was here!

Many children played under Elmwood Tree.
"Your leaves make shade," said
the children.

Flapper Bird made a nest in Elmwood.
"Your leaves hide my nest," said Flapper.

"The children like my leaves. Flapper Bird likes my leaves," said Elmwood.

A cool wind blew one day. Elmwood was sad. Elmwood said, "Summer is over. Soon I will have no leaves. The children will not come and play under me."

Flapper said, "The children
will return, Elmwood. The children
will come back. Wait."

Elmwood looked at the other trees.
The other trees had yellow and red leaves!

"The other trees have new colors,"
said Elmwood.

"You have new colors, too," said Flapper.

Flapper said, "I will fly to a warm place
now. You will stay here. Wait for
the children."

The next day, one red leaf fell from Elmwood. The leaf fluttered in the wind. The leaf went up and down. The leaf fell to the ground.

Then other leaves fell from
Elmwood Tree.

"My leaves are gone!" said Elmwood.
He was sad. Fall was here.

Then the children returned! The children jumped in Elmwood's crisp leaves.

Now Elmwood was happy. "The air is cool. But the children still like my leaves!" said Elmwood.